Hockey in the autumn.

PUFFIN BOOKS

The English Roses

Goodbye, Grace?

PUFFIN BOOKS

Published by the Penguin Group
Penguin Books Ltd, 80 Strand, London WC2R 0RL, England
Penguin Group (USA) Inc., 375 Hudson Street, New York, New York 10014, USA
Penguin Group (Canada), 90 Eglinton Avenue East, Suite 700, Toronto, Ontario, Canada M4P 2Y3
(a division of Pearson Penguin Canada Inc.)
Penguin Ireland, 25 St Stephen's Green, Dublin 2, Ireland (a division of Penguin Books Ltd)
Penguin Group (Australia), 250 Camberwell Road, Camberwell, Victoria 3124, Australia
(a division of Pearson Australia Group Pty Ltd)
Penguin Books India Pvt Ltd, 11 Community Centre, Panchsheel Park, New Delhi – 110 017, India
Penguin Group (NZ), 67 Apollo Drive, Mairangi Bay, Auckland 1310, New Zealand
(a division of Pearson New Zealand Ltd)
Penguin Books (South Africa) (Pty) Ltd, 24 Sturdee Avenue, Rosebank, Johannesburg 2196, South Africa

Penguin Books Ltd, Registered Offices: 80 Strand, London WC2R 0RL, England

puffinbooks.com

First published in the USA in 2007
Designed by Toshiya Masuda and produced by Callaway Arts & Entertainment
First published in Great Britain in Puffin Books 2008
1

Copyright © Madonna, 2007
All rights reserved

The moral right of the author and illustrator has been asserted

Fluffernutter is a registered trademark of Durkee-Mower, Inc. and is used by permission.
All rights reserved

Made and printed in Italy

British Library Cataloguing in Publication Data
A CIP catalogue record for this book is available from the British Library

ISBN: 978-0-141-38380-4

All of Madonna's proceeds from this book will be donated to
Raising Malawi (www.raisingmalawi.org), an orphan-care initiative.

Contents

CHAPTER I

A Shark in the Goldfish Bowl

too much T.V.

If you still have not heard of the English Roses, then I am very afraid, my dear, that you are watching too much television. Either that or you've got your nose stuck in some other book. Or perhaps you're spending all your time working on your dance moves. If it's the first reason, shame on you! If it's either of the other two, here's what I think: they are noble causes. But you really need to hear about these English Roses. I mean, they are something *else*.

Here is what they are not:

a. a famous painting

b. a new line of shoes

c. cupcakes

The English Roses *are* five girls named Nicole, Amy, Charlotte, Grace and Binah. They are best friends. I know it may *seem* hard to imagine five best friends, five different personalities with five different sets of likes and dislikes. The English Roses are not identical; they don't all think alike. They don't all dress alike. They don't all have similar families. But they do have one another. They support one another; they love one another; they laugh and dance and play together. So, while best friends usually come in twos, or maybe – once in a while – threes, the English Roses somehow make it work with five. Sure, they have been through some difficult times. Hasn't every friendship been tested?

Which brings us to the horrible thing that almost happened to the English Roses. Just when you think everything is going along swimmingly, somebody goes and throws a shark in the goldfish bowl!

CHAPTER 2

Hello, Year Eight!

It was just after the start of the school year. The summer holiday had been lovely, filled with endless days of fun for the girls: sleepovers, picnics, tea parties and dancing, along with shopping, trips to the zoo, volunteer work – the girls had given everything a try.

Now they were settling back into the whole school routine. They'd found their lockers, picked the perfect lunch table, and synchronized their hallway routines. Last year with Miss Fluffernutter had been a lot of work, but tons of fun too. They were happy with their new teacher, Mrs Moss, and were looking forward to conquering year eight, to giving it their special English Roses treatment.

At lunchtime, the five friends gathered at their usual table in the cafeteria, the one they had picked because it was close to the vending machines and even closer to the table where the cute boys in their year sat. Never one to sit still for more than thirteen seconds, Grace was eating an apple and juggling a football between her feet under the table.

What? Football? Oh, come on! You know I'm

talking about the kind of football where you actually kick the ball, right? What the daft Americans call soccer, although why they call it soccer I'll never know. It's a game played with feet, people; clearly football is a better name! Anyway...

'I can't wait for next weekend. It's a long one; we have no school on Monday!' Grace exclaimed around a giant bite of apple.

'I can't wait either,' cheered Amy, looking up from her sketchbook, in which she had been designing fabulous fashion creations ... as usual.

Binah, who was always the most practical of the girls, laughed. 'But school has just started! How can you already be thinking about a day off?'

'I've been thinking about it, too,' admitted Nicole. 'Especially during maths. Talk about boring!'

'What should we do?' Grace wondered.

'Didn't we discuss this right before school started?' Nicole wondered.

'Yes,' Charlotte said. 'I thought we'd agreed to a sleepover.'

'You're both right,' Binah said. 'We did, and I've already asked my dad for permission. I'm good to go!'

'Excellent!' shouted Nicole. 'Sleepover on the first night of the long weekend. Whose house? We could do it at mine, I guess, because my dad's travelling, so my mum will be happy for the company.'

'Travelling again?' said Charlotte. 'That's the second time this month.'

'Well, that's the life of a diplomat,' Nicole answered, chewing her nails as she always did when something bothered her. She was proud of her dad for representing England at important meetings all over the world, but she couldn't help feeling upset when he was away.

'Okay, Nicole, thanks!' Grace rushed in, for she could see that Nicole was starting to feel sad about her dad's absence. What was it with parents lately? Her own had been acting pretty strange too. 'Is Nicole's house okay for everyone?' she asked the others.

'Actually, mine is fine,' said Charlotte. 'Do you like that rhyme? I've already asked Nigella to prepare all kinds of yummy snacks for us.'

'Good,' said Grace, who, like the other Roses, had enjoyed many, many previous treats made by Charlotte's amazing chef. 'Because I don't think we can do it at my house. My mom's been straightening up and throwing things away for the past few weeks. She's really crazy these days about keeping the house clean. I don't think we would feel comfortable there; it's like we'd have to wash our hands before we touch anything. It's the strangest thing.'

And this is where all the trouble begins for the girls, although they don't quite know it yet. But I'm getting ahead of myself!

CHAPTER 3

You Know Parents!

'MOOOOOOM!' Grace yelled up the stairs. 'Can you hurry, please?! I'm going to be late to meet the girls!'

It was the very next day, Saturday, and Grace was in a hurry to get to the park to meet the other English Roses for their weekend gossip session. It was an event that she looked forward to every week. The girls liked to laze about in the sunshine, eating and talking and feeding the ducks. It was great fun to have time together uninterrupted, not worrying about school bells or anything. Grace didn't want to miss a minute of it.

A rustling sound came from upstairs. 'Just a second, Gracie,' Mrs Harrison called down. 'I know your jacket is around here somewhere; I saw it just the other day. It's too cold for you to be roaming around outside without a coat.'

Grace gave a giant sigh and shook her head. She didn't mean to be rude, but her mom had been so preoccupied and scatterbrained lately. She was constantly organizing and packing things away. Nothing ever seemed to be in the right place any more!

'Found it!' Grace's mum announced proudly as she ran down the stairs and handed her daughter the jacket. 'Now, have fun and be careful,' she said, kissing Grace on the forehead.

'Okay, I will, Mom,' Grace called as she bounded out the door. 'Bye!' Once she was outside, Grace broke into a run.

Ten minutes later, she arrived at the park to find all of the other Roses already seated on a blanket beneath their favourite tree. 'I'm so sorry that I'm late!' she said breathlessly. 'My mother insisted that I wear a jacket today, and then we couldn't find one anywhere. She's packed everything away. I swear, I don't even recognize our house any more!'

'It's okay, Grace,' said Binah loyally. 'We're just glad you're here.'

'But it's so odd,' Grace continued, frowning. 'Our house used to be a bit messy, but it was always comfy as flannel pyjamas. Now I can't find anything anywhere! Honestly, if I really want to know where something is, I hide it at the back of my wardrobe. That way, my mother won't find it and file it somewhere else. My brothers are going nuts too. They've never been sorted and labelled and organized before!'

'Don't worry,' said Nicole. 'Maybe your mother read an article on focusing her life.'

'Yes,' said Charlotte. 'Next thing you know, she'll be hiring a wardrobe organizer like my mum!'

Now, the English Roses all knew that Charlotte's family was wealthier than most. Charlotte usually took pains to hide that fact, but the other Roses liked to tease her about her posh charm-school ways. Still, Nicole couldn't help but note, 'Your mum hired someone to organize her wardrobes, Charlotte?! I didn't even know a service like that existed!'

'Oh, it exists, all right,' laughed Charlotte. 'If there's a service out there, my family knows all about it!'

'Don't fret, Grace,' Binah said. 'I'm sure your mum will grow out of this.'

'Yeah. You know parents,' Nicole added. 'Just when you think you've got them figured out, they're on to the next silly scheme!'

CHAPTER 4

Cute-Boy Alert!

Grace may have been a little put out by her
mother's new attitude towards housekeeping,
but all of those thoughts were soon pushed
out of her mind.

You see, on Saturday afternoons, Grace and her
brothers, twins Matthew and Michael, had a long-
standing ritual. Just after lunch, the three of them

changed into workout gear, pulled on their shin pads, laced up their boots, and headed to the park to play football. It didn't matter what the weather was like; if it was cold they wore sweats, and if it was hot they wore shorts and T-shirts. Grace and her brothers played through sweltering heat, freezing winds, torrential downpours, and fierce snow-storms. The only time you would not find Grace and her brothers on the football field on a Saturday afternoon was during a thunderstorm. Maybe.

'Hurry up, Grace!' urged Matthew.

'Yeah, Grace, move it along!' said Michael.

'Listen, you two,' Grace retorted. 'I can't help it if my legs are half as long as yours! You guys are walking too fast for me!' Which, naturally, just made her older brothers walk faster.

'If you weren't such a talented kicker, Grace, we'd have left you behind long ago,' Matthew teased.

'But you *know* you need me!' Grace teased right back.

'Yes, you do make us look good,' Michael answered. At sixteen, Matthew and Michael played in their own league but also coached Grace's

team. 'Lucky we worked so hard on you,' he continued. 'Now you're our secret weapon!'

Grace couldn't help but smile proudly at that. It
was true. Grace was a very talented footballer, in
part because of their coaching and in part because
of her own abilities. She was fast, agile, accurate,
and fearless – all great qualities for a forward.

'Hey, guys,' Grace said, changing the subject.
'What time do you think Dad will get here? I really

" ferocious foot "

want him to see my scissor kick; I'm getting really good.'

'We'll be the judge of that!' said Matthew. 'I guess Dad will show up later on, like he usually does.'

Though Dr Harrison was an orthopaedic surgeon and very busy, he tried to see all of Grace, Matthew and Michael's practices.

TWEEEEEET!

Matthew and Michael blew their whistles loudly. They were here to practise, and practise they would. No dillydallying. No idle chitchat. Grace charged out on to the field. Once the whistle blew, she was completely involved in the game. It made her a very good player and an extremely tough opponent.

Matthew and Michael's nickname for Grace was Ferocious Foot, and they gave that foot quite a workout! But she held her own during a tackle and seemed to be all over the field. She even managed to score three goals. At the end of practice, the Harrisons gave each other high fives.

'Nice job!' someone called out as Grace was gathering up her things: her sweatshirt, discarded early in the practice, and a water bottle.

Grace looked up to see a boy she didn't know, a boy who'd been talking to her brothers earlier. 'Thanks,' she said shyly.

'I'm Anthony Strong,' the boy said.

Grace's heart was pounding very loudly – and it was not from running around on the field. Her words, when they finally came out, were barely audible. 'I'm Grace,' she replied, sounding much squeakier than she would have liked. Great, she thought, now this guy would think she was a completely silly girl!

'Oh! I've heard about you. You're the Harrisons' little sister, right?'

'Yes,' Grace said, sounding more like her regular self. 'What do you mean you've heard about me?' she asked.

'I met your brothers this summer, when I moved to town. I sometimes play on their team, and I've heard them talk about you. You really are as good as they say.'

'Oh,' Grace said, and could feel herself blush. 'Thanks.'

'We'd better get going, Gracie.' Michael and Matthew came rushing up. 'Hey, Anthony,' they said together. Eyeing the football Anthony was holding, Matthew asked him if he was about to play.

'Yup,' answered Anthony. 'I want to get in some extra practice.'

'Look at that, Grace!' Michael teased. 'That's the kind of attitude we coaches look for in our players.'

Grace rolled her eyes at her brothers and smacked Michael lightly on the arm.

'See you,' she said to Anthony.

'Catch you around,' said Matthew.

'Don't forget that we're practising on Thursday night,' Michael said. 'It would be cool if you could play.'

'Awesome! See you then,' Anthony called.

Grace watched Anthony walk across the field. 'I don't remember seeing him around. Where is he from?' Grace oh-so-casually asked her brothers.

'He's new to the league this season,' Michael said. 'I think he's in your year, actually. He's a great player.'

'I haven't seen him at school,' Grace offered. 'Maybe he goes across town?'

Losing interest in the topic, her brother shrugged carelessly. After all, it's not as if it made any difference to *him*. All Michael cared to know about Anthony Strong was that he was a great footballer.

The cake sale is in full swing!

'I wonder what happened to Dad?' Grace wondered.

'What do you mean?' asked Matthew.

'Well, he never showed up,' Grace answered. 'I hope he's okay.'

'Don't be such a drama queen, Grace!' Matthew answered. 'So the man missed one practice; what's the big deal?'

Grace started to answer him back but then didn't speak. Her brothers clearly weren't interested. She had a few uncharitable thoughts about how clueless boys could be, then she thought more about Anthony. She was simply going to have to find out more about him on her own. Which she promised herself she would . . . with the help of four very dear friends, of course. Because if you've learned anything by now, you will recall that the English Roses are always there for one another. Always. That last thought made her smile as she trotted beside her brothers on the way back home.

CHAPTER 5

Five Minds Are Better Than One

Sunday afternoon found all five English Roses cleaning Binah's house. Now, you may think it odd that five girls would be willing to clean someone else's (never mind their own!) house on a lovely weekend afternoon. But if you think that about the English Roses, you clearly haven't been paying attention.

The English Roses are just different, and this is no ordinary friendship. Nope, the Roses are in this for the long haul, for good times and bad, for better or worse.

As you know, dear reader, Binah lives alone with her dad because her beloved mother is dead. Binah and her father do not have much; their things are threadbare and old, but Binah takes a lot of pride in keeping things nice for her little family. They may not have new clothes or new furniture or a fancy car, but what they do have is neat and clean and beautifully ironed.

All of this keeping-up-the-house used to take Binah hours and hours and hours, and she never had any time to play or just be a normal young lady. But that was before she became friends with the

English Roses. The English Roses are like the Three Musketeers: 'All for one and one for all' and all of that. Though it might seem strange to *you* that Amy, Grace, Nicole, and Charlotte would willingly give up free time to clean Binah's house, it does not seem in the slightest bit strange to them.

Binah's dad wasn't home. He had a big carpentry job going on and seemed to be working seven days a week lately. The girls had free rein of the house and used their time well. They stripped the beds of the sheets and washed them. They cleaned windows until they sparkled. They removed every bit of crockery from the pantry, wiped down all the shelves, and then reorganized. They mopped up the floors and scrubbed down the walls. All the while, music played and they danced and laughed and gossiped.

When Charlotte got a whiff of the cleaning solution Binah was using on the kitchen floor, she gasped, 'Wow! That's strong!' And that, of course, reminded Grace of her encounter on the football field with a certain Anthony Strong.

'Oh! You guys, I met a really nice boy at my football practice today. He plays with my brothers, and he told me that I was really good!' The other Roses couldn't seem to get enough information and asked their questions all at once.

'Where does he live?' Binah asked.

'Where does he go to school?' Charlotte wanted to know.

'Is he really cute?' Nicole wondered.

'What was he wearing?' Amy demanded. She firmly believed that a boy's outfit explained a lot about his personality.

Grace was laughing at their reactions and insisted, 'The important thing is that I had the most awesome corner kick and he saw it!'

'Oh, we're back to football?' asked Nicole. 'Yawn.'

'Okay, okay.' Grace laughed. 'Here's what I know: he's new in town, my brothers think he's a good guy, he's a great player himself, and he thinks I'm a brill player. And he's cute!' It wasn't easy admitting for the first time that you might like a boy, so Grace took a deep breath before blurting out, 'I need your help in finding out more about him.'

Realizing that Grace really was impressed by this boy, the English Roses immediately agreed to help.

'I'll do a search for him on my computer at home,' Charlotte said. 'You never know what you can find out about people!'

'That's our Charlie,' Amy giggled. 'Such a good spy.'

Nicole, who was usually the brains behind any operation, didn't want to be left out of this one. 'I'll ask some questions around school,' she offered. 'It'll be a good exercise in character development for the story I'm working on. Don't worry, I'll be very discreet!'

'And I'll ask my dad if he knows anything about a new family,' Binah chimed in. 'He's often got a project going on in town, so he sees a lot.'

Once that was all settled, Grace decided it was time to share her concerns about her parents with her friends. 'Guys, I'm a little worried about my parents. My dad didn't make it to our practice. That's not like him. Then, my mom was so weird yesterday when we got home from the field.' Grace began to speak in a much more serious tone. 'She was taking down some of the pictures on our walls.'

Amy could hear something different in Grace's voice and grew concerned. 'Okay, Gracie,' she said. 'Tell us again exactly what your parents have been doing.'

So Grace began her list (which, truly, wasn't very

long, but she had a bad feeling and feelings must be shared, especially with such good friends). 'Starting this summer, my mom has been really focused on our house. She's gone through each room, one by one, and thrown away huge boxes of papers and toys – everything we don't use any more. She donated bags and bags of our outgrown clothes and books we don't read any more. She nags us all the time to keep our rooms neat; our house really looks different these days.'

'What else has changed?' Charlotte wanted to know.

'Well, she keeps buying fresh flowers and leaving them in a vase on the dining-room table. Then, and I know this may seem like nothing, she's been baking cookies like there's no tomorrow – all different types; she says she's just trying out new recipes. But my mom is *not* the cooking-baking type. And my dad? He's always had a crazy work schedule. Being an orthopaedic surgeon is a tough job, I know that. But lately he's almost never around. Not showing up yesterday was so unusual.'

'What do you think it could be?' Binah questioned.

'I don't know,' Grace answered. 'Honestly, I haven't been paying too much attention until now. I spend most of my time thinking about football and school. Oh! Am I a terrible daughter?'

'No!' all the other English Roses chorused at once.

'But what if something is really wrong?' Grace asked.

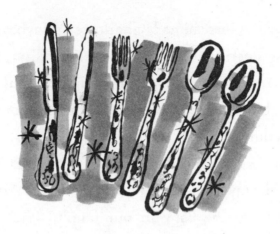

'Gracie, I'm sure everything is fine,' said Amy.
'Let's think about this. What could explain their
behaviour?'

There was silence for a moment as the girls
thought. Well, it wasn't really silent because there
was some excellent music in the background. The
girls couldn't keep their toes from tapping either.

'I know!' exclaimed Charlotte. 'Maybe you're getting a pet!'

'Wow!' said Grace. 'That would be fun! But I don't think that's it. We haven't talked about dogs or anything.'

'You don't think your mum is going to have a baby, like my mum, do you, Grace?' asked Amy.

'No! I'm the baby in our family,' Grace said. 'They tell me that all the time. My mom says that when I arrived on the scene, they broke the mould because they couldn't imagine a better child!' That thought made her smile; it always did.

Since Binah had such a wonderful relationship with her dad, she asked, 'Could you just ask your dad what's going on?'

'No,' Grace answered, and the smile left her face.

'His schedule has been so insane. And he's just left for an overnight trip to Paris for meetings. I couldn't possibly bother him with this while he's away.' Now Grace looked close to tears.

Nicole had had enough. 'Okay, Grace,' she said. 'If you can't ask your parents about this, we'll just have to figure out the mystery on our own. Your job is to watch your mum for clues while your dad is away.'

'Yes!' said Charlotte. 'Every time she does something unusual, you report back to us. We'll put our heads together and figure out what's up at the Harrison house.'

One by one, the English Roses gave Grace a big hug. And Grace was very grateful to her friends. 'Hey!' she said. 'All of this cleaning has made me

very hungry. Didn't you promise us tea, Binah?'
she asked.

The other Roses were not fooled for one minute.
They knew that Grace was still very upset about
her parents' behaviour. She was just trying to make
them all feel better by changing the subject. Each
English Rose silently promised herself to help
Grace feel better and, most of all, not alone.

Binah's tea was delicious! She and her dad might
not have a lot of food in their cupboards, but the
cucumber sandwiches she made for her friends
were the best any of them had ever tasted. Even
Charlotte, who'd eaten at the best restaurants in
London, couldn't remember enjoying tea more.

Grace started to feel better. Who wouldn't?
Everything in life looks more promising when
you're surrounded by friends who love you and
your belly is full of great food. As they munched,

the conversation turned back to Anthony, and that was a happy change for Grace.

CHAPTER 6

Miss Fluffernutter Strikes Again!

Monday morning dawned bright and clear. The English Roses gathered at the entrance to the school, eager to ask Grace about the rest of her weekend. But Grace had nothing new to report.

At lunchtime, the English Roses sat together and talked about their plans.

'You're still set for our sleepover, right, Grace?' asked Charlotte.

'Yes,' Grace answered. 'Or, at least I think we're okay. I haven't asked my mom about it since last week. I hope she doesn't change her mind.' Grace's eyes got a faraway look, and a little worry line formed on her forehead. All the Roses recog-nized the signs that Grace was anxious.

Nicole tried to get her to think about something happy. 'Have you seen Anthony around?'

Grace's face lit up. 'No.' She smiled.

'Tell us again what he looks like,' said Binah. 'This way we'll be sure to recognize him if we see him in the hallway.'

Well, that was all the prompting that Grace needed. As the Roses smiled and nodded in encouragement, Grace filled them in once again on all the details about Anthony. They were so involved with the description that they didn't even notice Miss Fluffernutter as she walked up to their table. And it wasn't easy to miss Miss Fluffernutter. The English Roses loved her because she was delightful and funny and kind. Also because she was offbeat and a tiny bit eccentric.

'How are we all doing, ladies?' she asked.

'Great, Miss Fluffernutter!' the English Roses answered as one. 'How are you today?'

'I am well, thank you. But I find myself in need of some volunteers for Thursday's event.'

'Event?' asked Binah. 'What event, Miss Fluffernutter?'

'You don't know?' Miss Fluffernutter asked,

with real surprise in her voice.

'No,' chorused the Roses. 'Please tell us!'

'Why, the Miss Fluffernutter First Annual Cake Sale for Charity,' she told them. 'I'm forming a new club, which I'm calling The Helping Hands. We're going to think of ways for students to help those less fortunate. The most important thing we are going to do is raise money for local charities.'

'Oh!' said Binah. 'What a great idea. Can I bake?'

'Yes,' said Miss Fluffernutter.

'Can I help to sell?' asked Charlotte.

'Absolutely,' said Miss Fluffernutter.

'Can I make posters?' asked Amy.

'Without a doubt,' answered Miss Fluffernutter.

'Can we help?' asked Nicole and Grace.

'I'm counting on you!' said Miss Fluffernutter. With that, she sat herself down at their table and they started discussing details of the cake sale. And that's what the Roses loved about Miss Fluffernutter. She listened as well as she spoke; she learned as well as she taught. Wouldn't it be just divine if all teachers were exactly like Miss Fluffernutter?

With her usual efficiency, Miss Fluffernutter divided up the chores. She had already recruited a group of students to put up the posters that Amy and others would make, so she needed the Roses' help with the baking. Nicole and Charlotte volunteered to bring cookies, Binah agreed to make two cakes, and Grace and Amy each offered to make brownies.

'Thank you so much for your help, girls,' Miss Fluffernutter said as she left them. 'I knew that I could count on you! Your contributions, added to what I've already collected, will help make this cake sale a great success. I promise that you will feel really good about helping those less fortunate than we are. It's important to give as well as you get. Right, girls?'

'Right, Miss Flufernutter,' the English Roses answered.

And as she walked away, the other Roses could see that Grace's mind had strayed far away from her family worries.

CHAPTER 7

Cake-Sale Blues

As they headed out of the canteen, the Roses could talk of nothing else but the cake sale.

'Miss Fluffernutter is so awesome,' sighed Nicole.

'And she's *fun!*' said Amy.

'She has such a big heart,' said Charlotte.

'You're right,' agreed Grace. 'I've never really

thought about doing anything to help other people; I mean, we're just kids.'

'Yes, we all have a lot,' said Binah, who truly didn't have much. But, Binah would have told you, she and her father had each other and enough food to eat and a warm and dry house in which to live. 'We'd better get planning. Thursday will be here before we know it!'

With that, the school bell rang and they rushed into their classroom.

When the English Roses set their mind to something, there is simply no stopping them. Do I know this from personal experience? No, not exactly, but remember how they were with Binah at first? I mean, Binah wasn't always a part of their group. But that was all due to the BIG GREEN MONSTER.

Once the girls realized that lovely Binah was as beautiful on the inside as on the outside they worked hard to tame the BIG GREEN MONSTER. After all, jealousy has no place among friends, has it?

Then there was the incident with Dominic de la Guardia when the other girls were unhappy with all the attention the gorgeous new boy was paying to Binah. But, again, the girls worked it all out. That's what they do. Once they realized how awfully they were acting, they stopped immediately and encouraged Binah. So, it should come as no great surprise that Thursday's cake sale was quite a success. Here's the way it went down . . .

All of the English Roses arrived at school on Thursday morning together, except for Grace, who hadn't been ready when they'd stopped at her house. They'd offered to wait, but her mom had said that Grace was still in the shower and they'd have to go on without her. The girls were surprised, but hurried to school laden with their baked goodies. They stopped short when they saw the cafeteria.

The Decorations Committee had done an unbelievable job transforming the school's cafeteria. Many tables had been pushed together against one wall, and they practically groaned under the weight of the food on them. The posters that Amy and other students had made were hanging outside the school and throughout the hallways, directing people to the cafeteria. Miss Fluffernutter had organized music throughout the day; sometimes the

school band would play, sometimes the chorus would sing, and sometimes a student DJ would keep the beat going. There were wicker baskets set up so that people could make additional donations. Clever Miss Fluffernutter had priced things so that people almost always ended up with change, and many tossed the coins into the baskets. School hadn't even started yet, and the cafeteria was a flurry of activity. Students were scheduled to work behind the tables all day long, rotating so that they wouldn't miss any of their classes. And the food! The enormous stainless-steel counters in the school's kitchen were completely covered with gaily wrapped baked goods of every variety. Cookies, brownies, cakes, tarts, fruit-shaped marzipan – stacked in rows three deep on every surface. The

Grace pours her heart out to the English Roses.

girls could hardly believe their eyes.

Miss Fluffernutter seemed to be everywhere at once, directing food donation drop-offs, passing out flyers about local charities, and encouraging people to buy more and more.

'I wonder where Grace could be?' Nicole asked.

'I can't believe she's missing this!' cried Binah.

Just as her friends were wondering where she was, Grace threw open the doors to Hampstead Elementary and trudged down the hall to the cafeteria. Hot tears stung her eyes. With every step, her heart felt heavier and heavier.

That morning had been the worst in her life. Well, maybe she was being a bit dramatic, but it could certainly be classified as horrible, no good, and very bad! She could hardly believe her eyes when she had skipped into her kitchen that morning, filled with excitement about the cake sale, and found the brownie ingredients and pan – greased pan! – she had left for her mom the night before still out, and empty. Her mother had forgotten to make the brownies she had promised for the bake sale!

Thoughts raced through Grace's head as she shuffled through the hallway. She couldn't bear the idea of letting Miss Fluffernutter down by not bringing what she had promised. But worse than that was the thought that her mother had forgotten about her! Her mother, who was always saying that there was no one in the world more important than Grace and her brothers – who, up until that point, had always been one step ahead of her in everything: always had her lunch made, always had her clothes freshly laundered and ironed – *her mother* had simply forgotten her. And she didn't even want to think about that *other* thing – the thing she had found on the computer. The thought of it sent a shiver down her spine.

Grace almost couldn't look her friends in the eyes when she finally caught up with them in the cafeteria.

'What's wrong, Grace?' asked Binah, visibly alarmed.

'Where are your brownies?' asked Amy.

At the sound of her friends' voices, Grace lost her composure. Her face crumpled as tears streamed down her cheeks. Instantly, the Roses surrounded their friend and moved off to a quiet corner in the hallway.

'It's okay, Grace; just tell us what's happened,' soothed Charlotte, patting Grace on the back and handing her a monogrammed handkerchief.

'Thith-ith a-a nightmare!' sobbed Grace.

'Try to calm down, Gracie, sweetie,' Amy comforted. 'Take a deep breath and just tell us everything!'

Grace took several deep breaths and wiped her cheeks with the back of her hand. 'I don't have my brownies. I'm so ashamed!'

'There's nothing to be ashamed of, Grace,' said Binah softly, grabbing Grace's hand. 'What happened to your brownies?'

'Nothing happened to my brownies,' wailed Grace, 'because there never *were* any brownies. My

mom forgot to make them!'

'It's okay, Grace,' Nicole reassured her. 'Miss Fluffernutter will understand.'

'She may understand,' sniffed Grace. 'But I don't! How could my mom forget about making my brownies? I even offered to make the brownies myself, last night, but she told me that it was too late and that she would make them for me. But this morning, when I came down for breakfast – no brownies! How could she forget?'

The other Roses were quiet with sympathy. Imagine your mother forgetting to make brownies for a cake sale? Even Binah, or maybe Binah especially, could see why Grace was so upset.

But Grace wasn't done yet. 'It gets worse,' she sniffled.

'What gets worse?' asked Nicole.

'My life!' cried Grace. She almost didn't want to say the words she knew she had to say to her friends. She took a deep breath and began, 'This morning, before I left for school, I decided to check my e-mail; I thought you guys might have sent me a message about the cake sale or something . . .'

'Yes, go on,' urged Binah.

'The computer was on,' Grace continued, 'but the screen was black. When I hit the space bar, the page that someone had left open came up. It said 'Kraft Property,' and there was a whole page of houses for sale!' Grace sniffed and hiccuped. Then she went on, 'What if I am moving?'

'Moving?' cried Amy, shaking her red curls in disbelief. 'But . . . you can't move!'

'Grace, that's impossible,' started Nicole. But just then, the morning bell rang. With no more time to talk, each girl gave Grace a big hug. They promised to discuss the matter more at lunch. Bravely, Grace marched herself into the cafeteria to confess to Miss Fluffernutter that she hadn't, in fact, brought anything for the cake sale.

Miss Fluffernutter took a long, hard look at Grace's tear-streaked face. She listened to Grace's made-up story about a football practice running late, leaving her no time to bake (for Grace really didn't want to admit to her teacher that her mother had simply forgotten about it). And then Miss Fluffernutter, who always seemed to know the right thing to say, said, 'Please don't worry about this, Grace. I know that you have a heart of gold and would do anything to help someone in need. I've seen how you act with your friends and with the other students and on the football field. In fact, you can still help today.'

'I can?' asked Grace in disbelief. 'How?'

'Why don't you come here during your lunch period and act as my special assistant? I have students scheduled to work behind the table selling, but I could use help with organizing and keeping the line running smoothly. Would you be willing to give up your lunch break for this?'

Grace thought hard. It was true that lunchtime was usually reserved for giggling and gossiping with her friends, which was loads of fun. But she really did want to help others – and spend time with Miss Fluffernutter, who she was sure would make her forget her troubles.

'Of course!' she said brightly. 'Thank you, Miss Fluffernutter! I'll see you at lunch.'

'Perfect! I can always count on my girls!' said Miss Flutternutter, and she fluttered away, humming a happy tune.

With that, Grace scampered off to class, feeling just a tiny bit better. She was determined to be the biggest helper that Miss Fluffernutter could imagine.

Now, Grace's determination usually showed itself on the football field; when she got a certain steely look in her eyes, you just knew she was going to score a goal. But that day it scored something else – better sales than Miss Fluffernutter could possibly have hoped for.

At lunchtime Grace showed up, as promised, while the other English Roses found their usual table. The line of people wanting to buy baked goodies never seemed to let up, so Grace was on her feet the whole time. She emptied the money boxes when they filled up, kept the tables fully stocked with food, answered questions and kept the queue organized. Like Miss Fluffernutter, she seemed to be everywhere at once. From their table, which had been pushed into a corner, the other Roses watched her and smiled. They knew that Grace was working hard and maybe (hopefully!) even forgetting about her fears.

'Wait a minute, look over there!' Nicole said, just

as she was about to bite into her sandwich. 'Who is that boy talking to Grace?'

'Where?' asked Binah, puzzled. The cafeteria was filled with students and people for the cake sale; it was hard to know who had caught Nicole's attention.

'Look, over there!' Nicole discreetly pointed. 'Right next to the cash box.'

Grace and a tall boy, about their age, stood talking at the table where purchases were rung up. He held an enormous cookie in one hand and was trying to help Grace tape up some loose streamers with the other.

'Oooh. He's a cutie!' said Charlotte.

'Is that Anthony?' wondered Amy.

'We'll find out!' said Charlotte.

As they watched, Grace and the mystery boy smiled at each other, then he gave a brief wave and headed out of the cafeteria. When they were sure that he was out of earshot, the Roses called out to Grace. When she heard her friends, she hurried over to their table.

'And who was that, Miss Grace?' Nicole asked with a mischievous glint in her eye.

Grace, her eyes sparkling and her cheeks flushed, had a big smile on her face. 'That was Anthony!' she told her friends. 'What do you think?'

'He's adorable!' the Roses said together.

'He's in our year, but he's in Mr Farburger's class,' Grace said. 'That's why we haven't seen him in school until now.'

'What were the two of you talking about?' asked Charlotte.

'He wanted to know all about the cake sale and what the money is going for and how he could help. He said he's going to ask Miss Fluffernutter about volunteering his time. He suggested that our football league could get involved. Isn't that a great idea?' Grace answered.

It was a great idea, and Miss Fluffernutter was very pleased when Grace told her about Anthony's suggestion. The cake sale was a huge success. The students had helped Miss Fluffernutter raise enough money to make a real difference to many local charities.

Miss Fluffernutter announced over the school's loudspeakers at the end of the day, 'You should all be very proud, and I am very grateful for your help. And remember,' she finished, 'I'll be asking for your help again this time next year!' The whole school could hear her gentle chuckle as she clicked off the microphone.

CHAPTER 8

The Shark Is Back

Throughout the day, while she helped with the cake sale, and even as she walked home with her friends, Grace wondered about her parents. She decided that she would simply have to ask her mom for the truth, once and for all. It was a good idea and a very brave

one, but Grace never got the chance. Her mom wasn't home when Grace got there. She'd left a note on the kitchen counter for Grace and her brothers, telling them that she and their dad had a hospital function that night and wouldn't be home until late. She'd left dinner for them to warm up and instructions to call her mobile phone if they had any questions.

After dinner, Grace did her homework, practised some football drills with her brothers outside and then headed upstairs to bed. Once she slipped between the cool sheets on her bed, she pushed all thoughts of moving out of her head. She recalled the events of her day, how it had started so horribly with the unmade brownies, but how she had been able to help anyway. She smiled at the thought

of Miss Fluffernutter and how she always seemed to know just what to do and what to say. Then she thought about Anthony, which made her smile grow even bigger. She slipped off to sleep to the sounds of her brothers in their room, thudding a football gently against their heads, the door, the bed, the wall or any other surface they could see. She had sweet dreams about Anthony, who had been so friendly and kind to her.

You know, it is a good thing that Grace had such lovely dreams, because life was about to take a turn for the ugly. You'll see what I mean. Just wait.

The next day started out innocently enough. The English Roses left their houses and found a

sparkling morning waiting. Grace's mum was still sleeping when Grace left for school, and her dad had already left for early rounds at the hospital. Grace wasn't able to talk to either of them.

Grace met up with the other English Roses at lunchtime.

'Try to get to my house by five o'clock,' Charlotte instructed. 'Nigella is planning to serve dinner promptly at six.'

The other girls giggled softly. 'Sounds great to me,' said Binah, who was secretly just delighted that she did not to have to cook another meal.

When Grace arrived home after school, she found the house empty. There was a note from her mum stuck under the vase of fresh flowers on the dining-room table. The note read:

Grace,

Your dad and I have another hospital function tonight. I'm sorry that we keep missing you! I know you've got a sleepover at Charlotte's tonight. Have fun and don't forget your toothbrush! I'll come over in the morning; I don't want you home too late. We've got a busy day tomorrow!

Love,

Mom

'Another function,' Grace grumbled under her breath. But she didn't want to lose that exquisite first-day-of-a-long-weekend,   sleepover-looming feeling, so she just concentrated on packing up her overnight bag.

Remember what I said earlier about someone throwing a shark in the goldfish bowl? Well, here comes that moment. Grace was all packed up and ready to go. She walked through her house, making sure all the lights were off. The rooms felt famil- iar – after all, this was the house where she'd lived most of her life – but strangely unfamiliar too. Room after room was spotless and tidy. The mounds of dirty clothes were missing from her broth- ers' room. The newspapers weren't strewn all over the porch. There were no dirty dishes in the kitchen sink, and the coffeepot wasn't still half full of this morning's coffee. But the worst was yet to come.

As Grace passed through the kitchen, she noticed a small stack of newspapers on the counter.

They looked out of place in the spotless house, so Grace decided to toss them into the recycling bin. As she picked them up, she glanced down at the top sheet of newsprint. She literally felt the blood drain from her face when she realized what she was looking at. First of all, it was *Le Monde*, the French newspaper. Secondly, Grace could make out enough French to know what she was looking at. It was the property section of the paper, and someone had gone through it with a red marker and circled several of the listings for Parisian apartments. Grace felt her heart sink down into her shoes as she realized what this had to mean.

Cue the scary music.

CHAPTER 9

Fairy Dust Saves the Day

After seeing the evidence right there on the kitchen counter, Grace grabbed her bag and rushed over to Charlotte's house. She couldn't even form a proper thought as she ran down the street. For the second time in a week, hot tears stung her face. She rang Charlotte's doorbell over and over until Winston, the Ginsbergs' butler, answered the door.

'Good evening, Winston,' Grace said, for she always tried to remember her manners. Even when her world appeared to be ending.

'Welcome, Grace!' Winston answered. 'You're the last to arrive. The other girls are all in Charlotte's room. Dinner will be served in one hour.'

'Thank you, Winston,' Grace answered, and up the stairs she ran to Charlotte's room, to the safety of her friends' company.

'You'll never guess what's happened now!' Grace cried as she stormed into Charlotte's room. Binah, Charlotte, Amy and Nicole were sprawled on the floor and draped over the beds in Charlotte's room. They'd been listening to music and chatting while waiting for Grace to arrive.

'What is it?' asked Nicole.

'I . . . I . . .' Grace could hardly even speak. Charlotte rushed over to comfort her friend and lead Grace to an overstuffed chair. She handed her a tissue to wipe her face. The other girls quickly surrounded Grace.

'My mom wasn't there when I got home from school,' Grace began. 'I'd already decided that I was just going to come out and ask her what's going on. My brothers weren't home either, because they had a special football practice. I found a note from my mom saying that she and my dad had another function at the hospital.'

'Okay,' said Nicole. 'So far, no big deal.'

'Yes,' said Grace. 'But then I found a bunch of

newspapers left out on the kitchen counter. They made the kitchen look messy, so I thought I should put them in the recycling bin . . .'

'What was there, Grace?' Binah asked quietly.

'It was . . . it was the Paris property section of *Le Monde*, and a whole bunch of the houses for sale had been circled with red ink!' Grace cried. 'My dad was just in Paris for meetings! I think we might be moving. What else could this mean?'

'It does explain your mum's cleaning,' Binah said. 'People always tidy up when they sell their houses. You're supposed to make your home look as simple and clean as possible, so buyers can imagine themselves and their stuff in your house.'

'That's true,' Nicole said. 'I saw it on a decorating show once.'

'Yes,' Charlotte added in a small, sad voice. 'And you're supposed to put fresh flowers around so that your home smells nice. It also explains the cookie baking. Freshly baked cookies smell so yummy; they're supposed to make people feel good about a house and want to buy it.'

'Oh my goodness!' Grace cried.

'And finally,' Amy finished, 'I really hate to say this, but maybe your dad was in Paris for a job interview.'

'Paris!' Grace cried. 'I can't move to Paris. I just can't. It's too far away!'

'Let's not panic,' Binah said calmly. You see, Binah had been through an awful lot in her short life, and she was really very wise. 'Let's figure out if there's something we can do.'

'What can I do?' Grace cried. 'If my family moves, I have to move with them. But I can't bear to be separated from you four! We're the English Roses!'

'Maybe we're wrong,' Nicole offered. 'After all, we don't know all the facts.'

'What do your brothers think?' Binah asked.

'My brothers?!' Grace snorted. 'They are completely clueless. They wouldn't notice a plane landing on our roof – unless it was carrying the entire Chelsea team!'

Then everyone began speaking at once. It was pandemonium, I tell you! What I won't tell you is every little detail of their conversations, because you've heard most of it before. And besides, the really interesting part is still coming up. Just know

Grace's family celebrates.

that the other Roses did their best to comfort Grace and to come up with a reasonable scenario that did NOT include her actually moving. Fortunately, they are very clever girls, and they discussed the issue all through their delicious dinner, all through the popcorn and snacks in Charlotte's room later, all through the various beauty treatments they performed on one another, while brushing their teeth and washing their faces, while changing into their pyjamas. When they finally fell asleep, in sleeping bags lined neatly on Charlotte's floor, they figured they had come up with a decent explanation. To be safe, they planned to ask Nicole's family if Grace could move to their house; just as a last resort, mind you!

That night, snuggled on Charlotte's floor, each

girl except Grace had an identical dream, and here is what they dreamed: just four of the English Roses were walking down the high street. Grace was missing, and this disturbed each girl in her dream. Really disturbed her. The four Roses were quietly talking and window-shopping. Each girl was sad and missed Grace, who had moved away.

'Why are you all so gloomy?' a voice asked.

P.S.: it's no secret
that the English Roses
all HaD PiNK
toothbrushes
(Natch)...

The girls jumped, for the voice had come from Amy's backpack. The other three girls turned to see a fairy godmother perched on the backpack. She was short and plump and very jolly-looking. But you know that already, don't you?

Charlotte found her voice first. 'We miss Grace!' she said.

The fairy godmother sniffed. 'Oooh, I think I

smell high tea. Scrumptious! Is anyone else hungry?'
she asked. 'Oh, never mind,' she continued. 'I'll get
something back at the office later.'

What? You didn't know that fairy godmothers
have offices? Well, where else would they get their
work done, you ninny?

'Listen,' she said. 'I know you're sad and that you
miss Grace. But what kind of friends were you
all anyway?'

'We were best friends!' answered Nicole. 'We
miss her, and we're not sure how to be the English
Roses without her!'

'Harrumph!' snorted the fairy godmother. 'Is that
your idea of best friendship? Do you think
that love dies when people are apart? If you wanted
to, you could be as close to Grace as ever!'

'How is that?' asked Binah. 'She lives so far away now.'

'Let's take a little trip,' said the fairy.

Binah was confused, but the other girls had been on one of the fairy's little trips, so they simply closed their eyes (and Binah followed suit) while she sprinkled them with fairy dust. You remember this part, right? At once, they were flitting and flying around the countryside. Their first stop was Grace's new apartment. They saw Grace in her room, sadly reading a book on her bed. They wanted to stop, but their fairy godmother wouldn't let them. 'We must keep moving,' she said. 'I haven't got all day to spend with you girls!'

Their second stop was the post office nearest Grace's new home. 'Do you four know what this place is?' the fairy asked impatiently.

'Yes,' the Roses answered.

'Good!' said the fairy. 'Here's a little tip. Why don't you help keep this place in business?'

'What do you mean?' asked Amy.

'What I mean,' started the fairy, and the girls could see that she was trying to be patient with them, 'is that you should write Grace letters. It's a fun way to keep in touch. What's better than getting mail?'

Before the girls could answer, the fairy whisked them off to the phone company headquarters.

'I know where we are!' said Charlotte.

'Good detective skills, Charlie,' said the fairy, 'but does anyone know *why* we're here?'

'Um, because we could call Grace?' asked Binah.

'Excellent!' cried the fairy. 'You were a very

valuable addition to this group. The others are not quite as swift on the uptake.'

Binah, Charlotte, Amy and Nicole laughed at this. None was offended, for they were used to the fairy's way of talking.

Finally, the fairy stopped at the train station. Before she could even speak, Nicole said, 'Ooooh! We could arrange a visit to Grace.'

'That's my girl!' said the fairy. The English Roses could see that, despite her occasional grumpiness, the fairy really was pleased with them.

As they touched back down on the far end of the high street, the fairy brushed the sparkly dust off their shoulders. She asked, 'Do you think that distance cancels the love you have for one another? Do you think that Grace is out of your lives? She's only as far away as you let her be. Now, if you will excuse me, I'm a very busy woman.'

In the blink of an eye, the English Roses were back in bed, fast asleep.

CHAPTER 10

Everything's Coming Up Roses

When they woke up in the morning, the girls told Grace all about their dream.

'Grace, we went to the post office,' said Binah. 'After that, we realized that we could send you cards and letters and packages all the time. We could send you pictures or jokes or just about anything at all!'

'The fairy godmother also made us stop at the telephone company,' added Charlotte. 'Of course we can call you every day!'

'Would you call me every morning?' asked Grace.

'Absolutely!' cried Nicole. 'Or maybe you should give me a wake-up call. You know how I am in the morning!'

Grace laughed at that, for Nicole notoriously did not like to wake up early. 'What else did you see?' she asked the others, eager to hear about their dream.

'Our last stop was the train station,' said Amy. 'We could all come and visit you at the weekend, or you could come and stay with us!'

'I love crossing the Channel!' Nicole cried.

'Oooh! I just thought about all the lovely shopping in Paris.' Charlotte sighed.

Grace was so happy to hear her friends talk like this. Even though the thought of moving terrified her, she began to realize that she wouldn't have to stop being an English Rose.

The other Roses told her that, no matter what happened, they would always be the English Roses. They told her they were 'all for one and one for all' and that she would never be alone, no matter how far away she moved. They made Grace feel so loved that she was ready for anything.

Which made the breakfast table surprise even more interesting.

As Nigella ladled out eggs and sausages, the doorbell rang.

'I'll get it!' cried Charlotte.

The Roses heard her voice at the front door, and then she came back into the dining room with Mrs Harrison in tow.

'Mom,' Grace asked, 'what are you doing here?'

'Oh, Gracie,' her mother said, as she gave each girl a big hug, saving the biggest hug for Grace. 'Didn't you hear me honking outside? I've been waiting for ages, and we have such a busy day today – I told you in my note, remember? I tried to call earlier, but the phone was busy.'

'Do I have to come right now?' asked Grace.

'Yes,' said her mom. 'Please gather your things.'

'I've put Grace's bag in the front hallway,

Mrs Harrison,' Winston told them.

'Thank you so much, Winston. That's very thoughtful,' said Grace's mom.

Grace slowly got up from her seat. She didn't want this moment to end. The other Roses could read her expression, and they all started talking at once, even though Mrs Harrison was right there.

'Don't worry, Grace,' said Binah. 'We love you!'

'Gracie,' said Amy. 'We'll still be as close as ever.'

'We'll write and call and visit!' cried Nicole.

All the girls gathered around to give Grace a big hug.

Mrs Harrison looked very confused, but she was in too much of a rush to ask any questions.

As they got into the car, she turned to Grace. 'What were the girls talking about?' she asked. 'Where do they think you're going?'

'Mom,' said Grace, taking a deep breath, 'it's okay, you don't have to hide it from me any more. I've figured it out.'

'Figured what out?' her mother asked, more confused than ever.

'That we're moving,' Grace said. Before her mother could say anything, she continued, 'But we've realized that our friendship will not be destroyed by distance. I can still be an English Rose even though we live far away, and –'

'Moving?' Mrs. Harrison interrupted. 'Who's moving?'

'We are,' answered Grace. 'Aren't we?'

'Why would you think that?' Mrs Harrison asked.

'Well, Dad's been gone so much lately, and the house has been so neat, and I saw those property ads . . . and those flowers . . . and . . . and –' Grace burst into tears.

'Okay, Gracie!' her mum consoled. 'Not another word until we get home. Your father and I have called a family meeting. He and your brothers are there waiting for us.'

'But, Mom –' started Grace.

'Don't cry, Gracie,' her mum said. 'Look, we're nearly home already. Let's find Dad and the boys.'

As soon as she and her mum walked into the house, her father caught Grace in a huge bear hug. 'There's my girl!' he said. 'I haven't seen you in ages. D'you think she's grown another inch?' he asked her mum.

'She looks exactly the same to me, Dad,' Matthew answered. He and Michael were draped over the living-room furniture, tossing a football back and forth.

'Can someone please explain what is going on?' Michael asked. 'We *are* going to make it to football practice this afternoon, right?'

'Yes, boys, you don't need to worry,' Mrs Harrison answered. 'Dad has some exciting news, and we called this family meeting to tell you about it.'

'Uh-oh,' Grace muttered quietly to herself.

'As you know,' her dad started, 'I've been to Paris quite a few times over the past several months.'

'You have?' asked Michael.

'Shush!' Mrs Harrison gently chided.

'Yes, Michael, I have,' Dr Harrison answered. 'I was actually recruited by one of the top hospitals in Paris; they want me to head up their orthopaedic surgery unit.'

'Cool!' said Matthew.

'That's a really long commute, Dad,' Michael warned.

'Yes, be that as it may,' said Dr Harrison, 'it is a very attractive offer, and your mom and I thought long and hard about moving to Paris.'

'Moving?' Michael and Matthew squeaked together.

'This would be a great move for your dad,' said Mrs Harrison. 'He's a very talented surgeon.'

Grace couldn't say anything; she just looked from her mom to her dad. What were they saying?

'However,' Dr Harrison said. 'Although it could have been an exciting opportunity for me, it seemed like an awful lot of disruption for our family. I decided to turn down the offer.'

'But there's more,' Mrs Harrison said, smiling at her husband.

'Yes,' he said. 'When London General heard that I might be leaving, they offered to make me head of orthopaedic surgery here.'

Grace shook her head to try and clear it. 'Wait, are you saying we're not moving?' she asked.

'That's what I'm saying,' her dad answered. 'We're not moving, but my new job will require even more of my time, at least initially. I hope you guys will be okay with that.'

'Dad!' Grace cried. 'I am sooo happy that we're not moving. I mean, I'm really proud of you and everything and I know you would have been great at the hospital in Paris, but I'm so glad we're staying!'

'Awesome, Dad,' said Matthew.

'Congrats, Dad,' said Michael. 'Now can we go to practice?'

'Sure.' Dr Harrison shrugged. 'Go on ahead, boys, and I'll catch up with you at the football field.'

As Michael and Matthew flew out the door, Grace ran over to give her dad a hug and a kiss. What wonderful, wonderful news. It was really the best of both worlds; her dad would get a new job, but she wouldn't have to move. She wouldn't have to be far away from the other Roses.

Mrs Harrison touched Grace on the shoulder. 'I think I owe you some brownies, honey,' she said.

Grace grinned. 'I'll help you!'

Grace and her mum baked quite a tasty batch of brownies that afternoon. As Grace bit into one,

she thought, *Mmm . . . the Roses must try this recipe!*

The Roses! How could she have forgotten?

Grace ran upstairs to her room and grabbed the phone. She had a few calls to make.

First, she called Charlotte. 'Hi, Winston, it's Grace. Could I please speak to Charlotte?'

When Charlotte came to the phone, Grace told her to hold on.

Then she dialled Amy's number.

'Amy! I'm glad you're home! I have something to tell you, but you have to wait a second.'

Then she dialled Nicole's number.

'Nikki dear! I have some news, but just hold on.'

Finally, she dialled Binah's number.

'Hey, Binah, it's me! Hold on.'

She pressed a button, and all five girls were connected.

'We're on conference!' Grace said. 'Girls, I just had to tell you all at once – WE AREN'T MOVING!!!'

There were shrieks and cheers from the other girls as they processed the news. When the excitement had died down, Nicole asked, 'So what's the explanation for those circled property ads then?'

'My dad was recruited by a hospital in Paris. My parents thought a lot about moving; it would be a great job for my dad. Then London General offered to make him head of orthopaedic surgery, so he gets a new job but we don't have to move!'

'Ah-ha!' the other girls chorused.

'I'm so glad you're staying, Grace,' Amy said. 'Because, truth be told, I am not much for the post office anyway. I'd rather see you face-to-face.'

'Me too!' Binah added.

'Me three!' Nicole chimed in.

'Me four!' Charlotte giggled.

Well, it looks like the English Roses are going to stay as tight as ever. But would you expect anything less from these five fabulous girls?

The End

MADONNA RITCHIE was born in Bay City, Michigan, and now lives in London and Los Angeles with her husband, movie director Guy Ritchie, and her children, Lola, Rocco and David. She has recorded 17 albums and appeared in 18 movies. This is the third in her series of chapter books. She has also written six picture books for children, starting with the international bestseller *The English Roses*, which was released in 40 languages and more than 100 countries.

PICTURE BOOKS:

The English Roses
Mr Peabody's Apples
Yakov and the Seven Thieves
The Adventures of Abdi
Lotsa de Casha
The English Roses: Too Good To Be True

CHAPTER BOOKS:

Friends for Life!
The New Girl
A Rose by Any Other Name

JEFFREY FULVIMARI was born in Akron, Ohio. He started colouring when he was two, and has never stopped. Soon after graduating from The Cooper Union in New York City, he began drawing for magazines and television commercials around the globe. He currently lives in a log cabin in upstate New York, and is happiest when surrounded by stacks of paper and magic markers.